CHASING DIVINITY (OLYMPUS LEGACY COLLECTION)

By

W.E. Hampton

Table of Contents

DEDICATION

For the people who helped me along the way. With countless hours of discussing or reading. The times when I seemed most difficult. Rayvin Bailey, Jason Tuiletufuga, Brian Cowell, Joshua Green, Dewayne Johnson, and Jacob Bell. Thank you for believing in me. To my wife and children who were with me from the very first page. Thank you for listening to my rants and changes to so many parts of this book. I wouldn't have gotten this far if not for all of you. To my readers, I hope you enjoy stepping into my world of fiction.

WRONG TURN

His heart raced as he crept along the silent, dark, corridor, straining to hear the slightest sound of someone approaching. Above Kai, the digital clock floated as it counted down with each step he took. 0:45:35.10......0:45:34:57. Fifteen minutes had passed since he had woken up. There was a note "ESCAPE BEFORE THE CLOCK REACHES ZERO!"

A faint harmonic humming flowed down the corridor. Soft and angelic, it erased all his fear. His mind going blank, and his limbs heavy. With a mind of their own his feet headed towards the beautiful voice. With each step, the ground shifted transforming, the cool, hard surface giving way to warm, tiny grains of sand. Tiny beads of weathered rock, slipped between his toes as he walked. Seagulls cried out overhead, their voices mingling with the enchanting melody. At the back of his mind something warned him to run, but each time he managed to break free. He was entranced with the song as it drew him closer. Waves beat against the shores of the beach like an impatient child seeking attention. Above him, seagulls called to each other. Strands of his hair swept into his eyes by the breeze blowing across his face. The sun bore down on him singeing his skin. His throat felt dry and ached slightly for the smallest drop of water.

"Come weary traveler, rest and let your troubles be washed away."

Hypnotized by the melody, his eyes grew heavy, and his feet again forced him towards the serene voice. A woman with long, flowing blonde hair sat next to a marble fountain with gold trim. Her eyes met his as she continued to sing.

"I have waited many lifetimes for the one who would come and rescue me. Come, weary traveler, rest and let your troubles be washed away."

If Kai had been in his right mind, he would have noticed the other men unmoving by the fountain. But he stumbled forward, to find the closest spot to the goddess. Her voice lulled him into a rhythmic sleep. Settling into a nice comfortable spot in the soft, warm sand. His eyes closed as the clock above his head ticked faster. 0:25:10.05....0:10:05:01.25....0:05:00.48

Calypso stopped singing and watched the young man fall asleep. A single tear slid down her face. She didn't like trapping anyone, but it was her punishment for helping the first mortal escape from her father. Stuck at this fountain and to sing until, one by one, their life expired. But if one man was to resist her voice and find his way out of the maze. Before the life clock counted down to zero. He could free her and the others. No man could resist her singing.

"When will my hero come to take me away? When will my heart be free? Come, weary traveler. Rest and let your troubles be washed away. I have waited many lifetimes for the one who would rescue me."

Calypso resumed the melody with a heaviness to the notes leaving her lungs. The labyrinth was alive and ever changing to confuse those who stumbled into its corridors. Her eyes landed on the young boy. His face was so peaceful and content as he slept his life away.

"Kai! Kai! WAKE UP!"

Startled awake, he opened his eyes to see a Goddess standing over him. Her eyes as blue as the cloudless sky above. For a second, he lost himself in her beautiful blue eyes.

"You must get up! Time is running out."

Confused, Kai sat up noticing the clock hovering not over his head as it had before. But over her head: 00:00:50.0.

"Kai!"

The urgency in her voice drew his attention back away from the dwindling clock. Fear gripped him, fear of the power she held over him. Kai turned and ran, not sure where he would go. But his only thought was he had to get away. Pumping his legs as hard as he could in the shifting sand. He continued to run until his feet met the hard stone floor of the St Michael's Preparatory School for Gifted Youth.

He was back. Daring a glance upwards, he noticed the clock was gone as well.

"Kai, why aren't you in class?" Mr. Greer, the Dean of students, called down the hall.

"I – I took a wrong turn Sir" he muttered slightly confused.

"Well, hurry along. Greek Mythology Studies is down the hall and to the left." Mr. Greer said, pointing over his shoulder.

Rushing off, he made it to the classroom just as the last bell rang for them to be in their seats. Kai sat down trying to make sense of everything. He barely heard the teacher calling his name.

"Kai! Are you paying attention? Turn to page 110 in your book."

He flipped through the pages until a picture of a blonde goddess sitting in front of a fountain caught his eye. A blonde goddess sat in front of a fountain. He stared opened mouthed at the picture. The woman in the picture bore a striking resemblance to Ms. Caly. His gaze shifted form the picture to Ms. Cal. The similarity was uncanny. Throughout the class, Kai found himself sneaking glances at Ms. Caly, trying to make sense of the connection between her and the girl. Today she wore her platinum-blonde hair in a tight bun. Her vibrant blue eyes shone brightly from behind her thin silver rimmed glasses.

Using the back of his hand he wiped the beads of sweat that gathered on his forehead. The A/C had gone out in the classroom again.

"Kai, you seemed distracted today. Is there something you would like to share with the class?" Ms. Caly called.

For a moment they're eyes met. Heat flooded his body. The loud pounding of his heart drowning out any other sound.

"No, Ms. Caly I was just thinking about the lesson." He stammered. "I uh, well I think Calypso's story about true love is stupid."

Several snickers erupted through the class. Sheepishly he glanced back to Ms. Caly. Entranced by Ms. Caly's static blue eyes, he continued.

"Like Calypso loved that mortal dude so she like gave up her life for his right? Look where it got her. All that mushy stuff? It's all made up right?"

"The mushy stuff." She smiled at him. "Is more real than you think." She explained before she delved back into her lecture. "

"Calypso cursed, unjustly by her father. Teaches us that love can have positive and negative effects. For she fell in love with a boy quite like yourself. Afraid of the mushy stuff. He wandered the Labyrinth for days without food or water. Until Calypso, the goddess of lost travelers, took pity on him and helped him. As punishment for helping him, Calypso lured unsuspecting men to their demise." Mrs. Cal said.

The class, intrigued by the story, all sat quietly on the edge of their seats waiting to hear more about this goddess of lost travelers.

"What happened to her?" a student in the back of the room asked timidly.

"She gave up her immortality to save one boy just as his life was ending. She could not bear to see such a bright young man die. Still, she watches over him even now." Mrs. Cal paused; her eyes lingered on Kai as she looked around the room.

For the smallest second Kai thought he could hear waves crashing on the beach. The slow ticking of a clock counting down.

"Ms. Caly, do you sing?" he said hazily.

She smiled at him. "I used to, but that was a long time ago," she said.

The bell rang breaking through the haze. He took his time gathering his things waiting to catch Ms. Caly alone. But he wasn't the only one interested in talking to Professor Caly. Shouldering his bag Kai left the room and made his way to the library in search of answers. The librarian who oddly resembled the school's patron Goddess Athena, handed Kai a withered book. The pages blank and crackling. About to return the book Kai stopped confused as ink filled the empty page.

"Calypso- the daughter of the Titan Atlas.
Cursed and imprisoned by the Gods for all eternity.
Embrace the love once forgotten.
To remove the curse, you must show true devotion.
Choose the path of courage, and let your spirit roam,
for in the face of love, no curse can find a home."

Closing the book, he rushed out of the library racing to find Ms. Caly. The faint melody echoed in his head as he pumped his legs faster. He had to make it this time. With each step, the ground shifted transforming, the cool, hard surface giving way to warm, tiny grains of sand. Tiny beads of weathered rock, slipped between his toes as he walked. Seagulls cried out overhead. The insistent ticking of the clock echoed in through the hall. At the end of the hall, she stood waiting platinum-blonde hair cascading down her shoulders. A smile on her face as she watched Kai race towards her.

END

WHISPERS OF THE WOODLANDS

Turning her face, Gaea soaked in the warmth from the sun peeking through the tall oak trees. A gentle breeze traced over her body, sending chills from her spine to her bare feet. Holding her hands out, she tried to catch the rays in her palms. She laughed at her own foolishness. Above her, the ear-piercing screech of an eagle rang out. As he challenged the other birds as lord of the sky.

Taking a deep breath, she felt the thrum of the forest calling to her. Surrendering to her instincts and the rhythm that flowed deep within her, Gaea raised her hands and flowed gracefully from one pose to the next of the dance of life. As she danced, the rhythmic sway of her hips caused sparks of red and gold to explode around her. The light wound itself into a sphere of swirling colors. Images of boy no older than eight sharpened as her body moved faster. He emerged out of a pyre of fire. His eyes matching the dancing flames. Shifting from red to yellow before settling on a mix of the two colors. His Hair crimson red hung loosely down his back Inspired, the image changed.

A small fissure formed in the middle of a volcano. Lava sprayed out in different directions. Burning away any traces of all it touched. A large brown hand shot out of the lava pulling away large chunks of charred earth. Arion watched in awe. Unlike the boy's birth this man's wasn't easy. He continued to claw until he made a hole large enough to pull himself through. His broad shoulders rolled and flexed as he stood to full height. He was a mountain of a man. Small patches of his thick black beard caught fire. Unfazed he raised one massive hand to pat the flames out. His eyes were unnerving, the left a bright orange glowed like the dying embers of a fire. Tiny speckle of brown floated around the iris. The right was the inverse of his left eye. A deep rich russet-brown with orange flecks of color. He raised a hand towards Gaea trying to reach through the roving sphere. Only to pull back at the last second.

Within Gaea, a fondness she couldn't explain for the two figures grew. Gaea twirled her hands summoning a second identical sphere. Side by side the images of the two beings floated. The edges of the two spheres brushed against each other. Sending a powerful wave of shearing heat rolling through the forest around her. Cosmic energy arched and surged around Gaea, Taking a life of its own. It reached out where the two spheres connected. Twisting violently through the air. Folding in on itself the light, faded to reveal a woman, a soft pink glow emanating from her. Beneath her feet remnants of scorched earth. A perfect blend of the two warring elements. Tall and regal like a queen, volcanic energy simmering beneath the surface. She was breath taking

Gaea felt a connection with each of them. As they took their first breath, so did she. They were alive as one. She heard their thoughts, felt their fear. Rustling off to the right distracted and severing her connection with them. As the animals that had gathered to watch her erupted into panic, fleeing in every direction. Men moving through the forest drew her attention. Against her consciousness, they left a filthy impression, though they were still several feet away from her.

Angry and disgusted that anyone would dare invade her forest. Gaea approached, intending to remove them. But one lone man caught her eye. She watched him leaning against the towering oak tree. His armor blending with the dappled sunlight filtering through the dense canopy above. Warriors, similarly, clad, formed a nervous ring whispering around him. The wind carried snatches of their conversations to her.

"They say there's a ghost in these woods."

"Haunted?"

"I'm too young to die."

On the opposite side of the forest, the Persian army, their gold banners reflecting the early rays of light against the verdant backdrop, waited with an unsettling stillness. Birdsong, once the dominant sound, dwindled to a hushed murmur. The wind, gentle as a lover's caress, carried with it the scent of earth and pine, masking the looming dread that hung in the air.

"Sire!" the spotter shouted.

From the shadows of the forest, a lone figure emerged, riding a powerful ebony steed. His banner, gold, billowed as if he carried the sun itself in the green sea of the woods. It was a challenge, that Euthydemus raced to meet. Their swords met in a resounding clash, the sound reverberating through the ancient trees like a call to arms.

The tranquility of the forest shattered. Arrows sliced through the canopy, finding their marks with deadly precision. Horses, like thundering tempests, charged through the underbrush, their hooves pounding a relentless rhythm. The clash of steel against steel echoed through the woodland, as warriors fought and fell amidst the ancient trees.

Their destinies entwined in the dance of blades and arrows. Fighting with a fierce determination that bordered on the wild. Euthydemus carved a path through the enemy lines. His sword slicing through all who dared stand before him.

The battle raged on, both sides fighting for control of her sacred woodland. An endless tide of enemies desperately trying to overwhelm him. For a moment, his vision was clear of any enemies. He glanced toward the edge of the ancient trees surrounding them.

Their eyes met. She heard him order his men to kill what he assumed was a spy. Several men moved forward: swords drawn. Calmly, Gaea stepped out of from behind the tree line, unafraid of the swords pointed at her. The air seemed to shimmer as if the very atmosphere recognized her presence.

In that fleeting moment, time itself held its breath. As she moved, her form seemed to shift like liquid moonlight, graceful and ethereal. Her presence carried a weight, both profound and humbling, as if the very earth acknowledged her as its custodian. Her hair, an unnatural color for a Greek woman. Wild and untamable forest-green curls dangled just past her shoulders.

A gentle, rich lilac aroma clung to her. Freckles adorned her amber cheekbones. With each step, the world around her responded. Flowers unfurled in her path, birds hushed their melodies in reverence, and the wind whispered secrets of distant realms. The elements themselves paid homage to her. A luminescent aura surrounded her, a halo of iridescent light that defied mortal comprehension.

Her eyes, pools of endless wisdom and ancient knowledge, gazed with a depth that touched the soul. They held the secrets of a thousand worlds and the mysteries of eternity. Harlequin- green timeless eyes held him entranced. Her ancient eyes were unlike any he had ever seen. They watched him with judging and contempt. As if she knew the thoughts he tried to hide from his men.

She tensed as she felt their eyes undressing her, desperate to see and taste her flesh. Her chiton slipped off her shoulder slightly, unsettled by her movements—exposing her tattoo. Fear and anger welled inside her at the thoughts she knew were going through their minds. She had seen the heated stares the men had passed over her body.

Around them, the forest came alive, and trees leaned closer to the men blocking out the sun. The surrounding forest grew dark and cold. Branches sharper than the eagle's talons crept ever closer. Desperate to claw and rip the men apart who invaded their domain and made their friend angry. Gaea stood, unaware of the impending danger to them.

Images of the guards being ripped apart by the trees danced in her mind. Gaea turned to face the men with petrified looks on their faces. The forest calmed as well when she wrestled her emotions under control. Trees returned to merely swaying in the wind.

Gaea smiled warmly at the men despite their fear-filled stares. They gave her a wide berth, eyeing the trees nervously, expecting them to come back to life. She blinked, turning away, releasing him from her powerful gaze.

"What is your name?" Euthydemus roared.

Her voice was a symphony of celestial notes, resonating with the harmony of the universe. Each word she spoke was a tapestry of meanings. Layers of understanding woven into a singular utterance.

"Gaea," she said in a soft, magical voice.

The men surrounding her shifted nervously. Her aura filling them with a potent mixture of awe, reverence, and an overwhelming sense of fear. It was as if, in that moment, the chasm between the mortal and the divine had opened, and in that realization, a profound transformation began. His breathing heavy, Euthydemus leaned forward in his saddle. His hand gripped his sword, drawing it halfway out of its sheath.

"My Lord?" The sergeant of his guard faltered, noticing the crazed expression on his face.

Shaking himself, he returned his sword to its sheath. A sense of relief washed over him as the adrenaline-fueled tension in his body slowly dissipated. Shaken by her sudden appearance amid the chaotic battlefield.

"Bring her and retreat," he said, his voice now more composed, yet still carrying a trace of urgency. Around them, the call to retreat echoed through the ranks of his army.

Euthydemus spun his horse around quickly, putting some distance between them. Making their way back to the castle, the sound of clattering of hooves on the cobblestone replaced the echoes of men succumbing to their wounds. Inside the castle, Euthydemus placed Gaea in a chamber, far from any other man, and allowed no one near her.

She could not roam the castle or speak with anyone. Around the castle, a hushed unease flooded the halls, as word of her ethereal appearance and the tattoo on her back spread. The inked depiction portrayed a woman gracefully dancing through the moon's phases, symbolizing new life. King Euthydemus kept Gaea locked in her chambers unless they had supper together.

She hated being confined to just the four walls of her room. Many times, she tried to escape, yet the power of the forest no longer flowed in her veins. They beat her severely each time she attempted to leave. Eventually, she accepted that her life now belonged to Euthydemus.

Several years passed, and Gaea though she didn't age, her body grew weak. Her skin dried out, losing its radiant glow. Disgusted with her lack of beauty, Euthydemus ordered his men to return her to the forest and leave her there. Entering the forest brought her back to life. Before the guards' eyes, her skin regained its angelic glow. She remembered watching one guard race away, returning with the king.

He quickly returned, eager to show Euthydemus how she had recovered. Believing it was a trick, King Euthydemus questioned each of his men, but each man gave the same account. The deeper they went into the forest; the healthier Gaea became.

Gaea quickly mounted her horse to return to her prison. Though she now had the freedom to return to the forest under supervision. She could return only for the briefest of times. If she tried to run or stay longer. Euthydemus ordered Her guards to burn the forest. Twenty men went into the forest with her, while more waited, ready to set fire to her forest.

Galloping away, Gaea's heart sank. When she returned to the estate, they would lock her in her room. There would be no plants to keep her company. Tears slid down her face the closer they got to the estate. Was this all she had to look forward to in life? Surrounded by four walls and forced to interact with men who wanted her body for their own selfish needs?

She wanted to be free to roam deep in the forest and not have to speak to a single person. To dance among the trees and feel the soft grass under her toes. Why couldn't they have left her there instead of forcing her into this life of captivity? Glancing back as they rode forward Gaea, thought she saw a boy running behind them through the trees keeping pace with the galloping horses.

A large golden eagle tucked his wings in before landing and assuming the shape of a man. Hidden behind a large oak tree, Uranis stood mesmerized by the beautiful young woman with wild forest-green hair. He waited and watched from afar for her to come. Serene and untamed, she was stunning to watch.

The graceful movements as she danced to a beat only, she could hear stirred something inside of him. His body burned with need. He longed to feel her soft amber skin. Uranis wanted to approach her, but he had never spoken to another person. Whenever he worked up the courage to approach her, she always left with the men wearing strange clothes.

Shiny pieces of cloth blinding him when the sun bounced off them. Even more strange, they choose to cover up the parts of their bodies that showed them to be male. Uranis glanced down at his own member, covered only by a loincloth. He wondered why they would hide themselves.

He noticed how the men watched her with the same burning desire he had whenever he watched her. It made his stomach turn to see such boldness and the things he had heard them whisper to each other. He was ignorant of some things they mentioned; he knew he didn't like it.

He glanced back at the woman. The garment she wore did little to hide her features from any of their eyes. The swell of her breast as she laughed at the birds. She had the smallest amount of hair between her legs.

Uranis stood watching as the trees came alive to attack the men. The entire forest responded to her anger. Branches and twigs started intertwining around his ankles as well. As quickly as the forest came alive, everything returned to normal. The girl appeared calmer. She turned to speak to the men, revealing her exposed back.

It was then he saw for the first time a tattoo on her back. As often as he watched her, he never paid attention to her back until now. A symbol of a woman with her arms raised as if she was dancing. The tattoo contained a language he had never seen before read—Gaea, mother earth, creator of life.

They mounted their horses, heading back the way they came at a hurried pace. The men followed behind her with sober expressions. Following close behind, using the trees to conceal his presence, Uranis easily kept pace with the horses as they galloped back to the stone fortress. Uranis watched as she wilted inside herself the further, she went into the stone walls.

The sad, defeated look she wore caused pain in his chest. His heart felt like it was being ripped in half. Uranis glanced down at his chest, expecting to see a wound. It hurt so much, there was no wound. The pain and sadness must be coming from the girl he had watched in the forest.

Needing to understand why he could feel her sadness, Uranis walked out from under the cover of the trees. Intending to speak only to her. He walked through the gates and was quickly stopped and surrounded by more men covered in metal.

"Halt! State your purpose!" the biggest of the men barked at him.

Uranis ignored him and continued towards the entrance he had seen Gaea disappear into. The sound of air whooshing behind him caught his attention. Spinning around, Uranis caught the blade aimed at his head. The distraction cost him. They had him surrounded now, swords drawn and aimed at his throat. One man, even to Uranis in height, stormed up, backhanding him. Pain exploded across his face.

"Put him in chains. He can wait for his highness to return to decide what's to be done with him." Barked the same gravelly voice.

Uranis was dragged away, the harsh rasp of his bare skin against the unforgiving stone floor echoing through the corridor. The guards, indifferent to his pain, flung him into a windowless cell. As the heavy door slammed shut, panic seized Uranis. The oppressive darkness closed in on him, and he craved the touch of open air on his skin.

Within the cramped confines of the cell, small creatures scuttled in the shadows, their movements barely audible. Desperation drove Uranis to hurl himself at the unyielding door. the impact sending shockwaves of pain through is body. He persisted, each futile attempt wearing down his strength.

Weaker now, he collapsed to the cold floor, resigned to the impending death that clawed at him. His thoughts drifted to the girl from the woods, a flicker of warmth in the encroaching darkness. There was something enchanting about her that had drawn him in. Determination kindled within him— if he survived, he vowed to find a way to speak to her.

THE SOUND OF THE DOOR opening startled Uranis awake. He didn't remember falling asleep. He must have drifted off in his weakened state. Light flooding into his cell burned his eyes. Raising a hand to shield them. Uranis squinted at the man standing in the doorway. King Euthydemus eyed the boy in the cell with revulsion.

The boy's head brushed the ceiling of the cell as he stood to face him. His ancient sky-blue eyes swirled with knowledge and judgement. King Euthydemus hated how those eyes made him feel. Judging him, as if they could read his every soul. Seeing the filthy state, the boy was in gave the King some satisfaction. Why his men even bothered him with trivial matters, as a beggar sneaking in was beyond him.

"Throw him back in the gutter he came from, make sure I am not disturbed again." the King ordered.

The guards moved forward, grabbing a hold of Uranis, not caring how their hands dug into his flesh. He said nothing as they pulled him out of the door. Though he was taller than the men dragging him, he was too weak to fight their hold on him. As he passed by a window and the sun briefly touched his skin. His skin and hair regained their natural color and felt stronger. Unfortunately, Uranis wasn't the only one who noticed the change in him.

King Euthydemus glanced at. Uranis as they drug him away. His eyes landed on the boy's back, and he saw — the large tattoo of an eye with a star resting between the boy's shoulder blades. The sudden change in the boy's appearance didn't escape his notice, either.

"WAIT!" the command rang out from where he stood at the cell door.

His guards paused; afraid they had not moved fast enough before incurring the king's wrath. "Sire?"

He said nothing as he approached them with quick strides. His hands rudely inspecting the tattoo on Uranis' back. Certain he already knew the answer, King Euthydemus still asked, "Where did you get this mark, boy?"

Uranis glanced over his shoulder from where he still knelt uncomfortably between the guards. **"Den katalaveno**—*I do not understand."*

Euthydemus stared blankly at the boy. The language the boy spoke sounded pleasantly like music. It wasn't one he was familiar with. Glancing at his guards, he hoped one of them understood, but he saw the same look of confusion on their faces. Grabbing Uranis violently by his hair, the king pulled Uranis towards him.

"ANSWER ME BOY! WHY DO YOU BARE THAT MARKING?" King Euthydemus roared at him, yanking his head around. Struggling to form the words in their language, Uranis latched onto the one word he understood.

"Gaea."

Hearing Gaea's name, Euthydemus flew into a jealous rage. Slamming Uranis's head into the wall. Was this boy sent here from a neighboring country to steal Gaea? He needed to know was Gaea was in danger. This boy would not take her from him. Wanting answers.

Euthydemus ordered his men to take the boy to the dungeon and beat him until he gave up who sent him here for Gaea.

For hours, they beat him in the windowless room, lit only by the torches in the room. When they first began beating him, Uranis's blood was golden and the wounds they inflicted healed immediately. The longer he stayed in the dark room, his blood turned black, the slashes stayed and deepened.

Every inch of Uranis's body ached and bled. He didn't speak their language, so he couldn't give them any answer other than the one word he knew. With each slash of the whip, he screamed out Gaea's' name. Which only made the strikes come harder.

IN HER ROOM, GAEA SCREAMED out as her back split open from the sting of a whip. For the past hour, Gaea had felt pains in different areas of her body. Was she going mad? There was no one in the room with her, and yet she ached and bled golden blood from injuries on her back. Her body shaking and covered with blood and sweat, Gaea stood unsteadily to her feet.

If she could just make it to the door, then one of her attendants could get help. She made it only a few steps before her knees gave out. Forcing her to fall breathing heavily as her back bled more.

At that moment, the King and several of his guards burst into Gaea's room. Euthydemus stared, horrified, at the amount of blood spilling out of her back. "FETCH THE PHSYCIANS IMMEDIATELY!" he roared to one of the maiden attendants. Euthydemus stepping closer, covering his mouth with the hem of his chlamys, he didn't want whatever afflicted Gaea to seize him.

The physician arrived, breathing hard. He bowed to King Euthydemus before seeing to Gaea. He poked and prodded the open wounds on her back. Gaea screamed each time his fingers went into her flesh.

"Highness, has the lady endured punishment?" he asked, still examining her back. "Her wounds are consistent with that of a whip."

Gaea hadn't received a beating in years. Since he had allowed her time to visit the forest, they found her in. It couldn't be a coincidence the boy bearing a similar marking as Gaea.

Turning quickly, the King raced down the stairs leading from Gaea's room with guards on his heels. Hoping he would make it before it was too late. He had to make it to the dungeon.

A WOMAN'S VOICE SCREAMING frantically drew Uranis' attention. He did not recognize the woman's voice in his ear.

"Zion! Zion WAKE UP PLEASE I CANNOT LOSE YOU TOO!"

Chained to the wall, Uranis turned his head to see who the voice could belong to. No one except the male guards stood before him.

"Zion!"

The whip whistled through the air, slashing his chest. Pain erupted as the whip struck virgin flesh.

"CLEAR! HIT HIM ONE MORE TIME. COME ON, YOUNG MAN, DON'T DIE ON ME!"

Tears Uranis held back spilled over and a man with grey hair and a strangely shaped face appeared in front of him. Was he here to take Uranis to the afterlife? What was happening to him? Another blow and more pain.

The guard raised the whip to strike him again. The door to the dungeon burst open, slamming into the cell wall.

"STOP!" King Euthydemus' voice rang out.

The guards immediately going to their knees as the King strode in the down the steps of the cell.

No one spoke as he examined the boy. He was barely alive. His blood, like Gaea's, was turning black. Euthydemus curled his lip in disgust. If it wasn't for his precious Gaea, he would let the beating continue.

"Take him down and see that he receives treatment for his wounds immediately." Euthydemus said, turning away from the dungeon.

The guards hurried to obey his orders. As they lowered him to the ground, Uranis surrendered himself to the empty void that awaited him. His last thoughts were full of regret. He would die without ever speaking to the beautiful girl. No, Gaea. Her name was Gaea, the dancing lady.

INTO THE ABYSS

Zion's eyes flew open just as the paramedics readied the defibrillator to shock him again. His chest ached and throbbed as he struggled to breathe through the pain.

Disoriented and frantic, Zion glanced around the room, searching for the boy Uranis, who he just watched being tortured. No, he thought, confused. He had felt every lash as if it was his body being beaten. Only the concerned faces of the paramedics greeted him.

"Where is Uranis?... He was dying. WE HAVE TO HELP HIM!" the panic in his voice alarming the adults.

His mother and the paramedics stared blankly at him. One female medic knelt next to Zion, drawing him into her warm embrace. She hugged him tightly to her breast, whispering in his ear so only he could hear.

"Shhhh, it's okay... do not worry about the past." Her soft voice soothed and drove the anxiety that had built up inside of him. Zion felt the woman's body shaking profusely and her silent sobs on his back.

Why was she crying? She didn't know him, but her embrace felt warm and familiar. Her arms hugged him tighter, Michelle rushed forward, roughly yanking him out of her arms. "What do you think you're doing with my son?"

The woman tucked her head as she wiped away the tears that fell down her cheeks before standing to face his mother. "I'm sorry I got a little emotional when I saw him lying there."

Her soft reply to disarmed Michelle's attitude. This woman was showing more concern for her son than she was. Maybe she was being too harsh by pulling Zion out of the woman's arms.

After all, she and the other medics in the room had worked hard to save him. While she just stood there crying for him not to leave her.

A tall blonde man strode into the room wearing the same emergency uniform. He angrily strode towards the female paramedic. Placing himself in front of Michelle and Zion. He stood as if to protect them from the woman. His aggression towards the female paramedic surprised Michelle. She took several steps back, pulling Zion with her.

In a deep baritone voice, he addressed the woman, "Nike, what are you doing here?"

She smiled politely at Zion and Michelle. "I was just leaving now that I know this young man is ok."

The male medic didn't relax his ridged stance until she was completely out of sight. He turned to face Zion and his eyes flashed magenta before going back to their normal skye blue. Afraid of the unnatural eye color he had seen, Zion looked away.

A woman's voice spoke in Zion's head. "Aww little human, are you scared? Let me give you a taste of genuine fear." The sinister smile parting his lips was the only sign the voice in Zion's head came from the man standing in front of him.

Before his eyes, the man's body morphed into a cobra with three heads spitting purple fire. The hair on his mother's skin grew sharp and prickly. She had more arms than before. Her body expanded, and she shifted into a giant spider. Acid dripped from her mandibles as she scuttled towards him, hungry for his flesh. Zion threw his arms up to protect himself, screaming for help.

"Zion! why are you screaming? What is wrong with you?" His mother's normal voice made him jump. Hesitantly, Zion lowered his hands, afraid it was a trick. Sobbing uncontrollably, he refused to answer his mother. The deep voice of the male medic cut through his hysteria. "Excuse me, ma'am, do you mind if I say something?"

Michelle nodded her head, stepping back to give him a clear path to Zion.

"Are you afraid, little guy?" he chuckled softly. Reaching his hand towards Zion. The gruesome images of Zion's mother transforming into a giant spider flashed across his mind. Zion pressed himself into the wall, trying to escape as far away from the man's outstretched hand. "He may be a little disoriented for a little while. He hit his head pretty hard."

Turning so only Zion could see his face. The man smiled before his face shifted, exposing the large mandibles hidden inside his mouth. He scooted closer, clicking them together. Screaming for his life, Zion covered his face. Praying that it would all go away.

"Honestly, Zion what has gotten into you? This nice man saved your life, and this is how you treat him? ... I'm sorry I didn't get your name?"

He turned, flashing her a dazzling, charming smile, stretching his hand out. " David Pittman ma'am." Michelle's face grew warm and pink from blushing. David was extremely handsome. His body rippled with well-defined muscle. Heat flooded Michelle's face, her eyes traveling up and down his body.

"I uhm... I thank you for saving my ...my son." She said, stumbling over her words.

David smiled another charming smile and nodded to her before following the rest of the paramedics out the door. Michelle stood in a daze, watching David leave. She watched him leave noticing how his body filled the uniform perfectly. She felt compelled to follow him. The sound of sniffling distracted her from thoughts of chasing after David.

Fed up with her eleven-year-old son crying again. Michelle grabbed Zion by his collar. He needed to stop acting pathetic and weak.

"ENOUGH CRYING! YOU ARE NOT A BABY!"

Tears fell faster down his face, staring up into the eyes of his mother filled with contempt and anger. She hated him. What had he done for her to hate him? Michelle couldn't take it anymore. Raising her hand, she slapped him, once and then again, and again, until he finally stopped crying. It should have horrified her how hard her hand fell repeatedly on his face. She felt nothing. Only pure bliss at seeing how much pain she caused him.

Why did she have to get stuck with his child while Patrick got to be high somewhere? She should leave him here, just like Patrick left her. No, she wouldn't be irresponsible like his father. "Get your coat and get in the car."

Sniffling, Zion rose slowly from the floor to head back to the opened closet and grab his coat. He wanted to ask his mom why he in trouble was; he was afraid she would hit him again.

She got in the car, slamming her door. Michelle glancing in her mirror briefly, glimpsing the bruises and busted lip she had given him. Was she treating him too harsh? The thought played across her mind. Again, a seductive voice entered her mind.

"No, it's all his fault. If he had been a better son, Patrick wouldn't have left you."

Michelle agreed with the voice in her head. Zion deserved to be punished for being a terrible son and causing Patrick to leave. Gritting her teeth, Michelle drove them away from their home in Charleston, South Carolina.

For nine-hours, they drove in silence, only stopping for fuel and quick bathroom breaks. Zion's stomach growled repeatedly; he dared not ask his mother to stop. He kept his eyes out of the window, watching the trees fade away into buildings. He read the sign just as they passed by. *"Welcome to Indiana Crossroads of America. Lincoln's boyhood Home."*

His mother drove until she found a cheap motel for them to stay end. There was only one bed and a raggedy old chair. Without a word to him, Michelle got in the bed and fell asleep. Leaving Zion to stay up alone in the uncomfortable chair.

ZION DREW HIS KNEES up to his chest, afraid if he fell asleep, his mother would transform into a giant spider again. Flinching every time, she shifted in her sleep. His eyes grew heavy, every creak from the bed and his eyes shot back open.

His eyes were finally too heavy to lift. Zion drifted off to sleep. In his dreams, he heard the same female voice from his living room.

"Aww little human, you thought I wouldn't find you. How about we have some fun?" her voice echoed all around him.

His mother transformed again, and her body had grown larger. Eight barbed legs scuttled forward, mouth frothing. There was nowhere for him to run. The spider grabbed him up in her mandibles, ripping his body in half. He was still alive. Zion felt his legs twitching, blood poured from his insides. Clicking her mandibles, his mother opened her mouth, swallowing the top portion of his body. Before he realized what happened, his body was back together. Only this time, Zion was sitting in the middle of a forest.

A woman's maniacal laugh filled the air. His mother burst through the trees. Again and again, the giant spider that used to be his mother killed him. Each time differently. Over and over Zion screamed for help, begged the woman to make it stop. Her continuous laughter was the only answer he got in return. His dream changed from the forest. He was now on a boat in the middle of the ocean. The water fiercely tossing the boat back and forth. His knuckles were white as he tightly gripped the bench beneath him.

Thunder boomed overhead and lightning struck the water. A wall of water slammed into the tiny boat, sending him overboard. His clothes were too heavy. Zion sank into the dark, bottomless water. His lungs burning for air. Just like with the spider, once he died, she revived him. Only for him to die again. When would this nightmare end? He couldn't take it anymore. The woman found new ways to terrify and kill him. Chased by lions and eaten alive. Set on fire. Beaten and left for dead.

He gave up trying to run or wake himself up, choosing instead to curl into a ball and wait for whatever gruesome death awaited him.

"Zion! Zion! ... wake up hunny. You've been screaming in your sleep." His mother said, shaking him awake. Staring wild-eyed around his bedroom before it registered, he was finally safe. He hugged his mother, squeezing her tight as tears ran freely.

"What's a matter pumpkin? Did you have a bad dream?" she said, rubbing his back, letting him sob into her shirt. His body shook uncontrollably. He couldn't stop crying to answer. She held him tight to her barbed body. Glancing up, Zion saw his mother's body expanding. She grew six more arms. He saw his panicked reflections in eight pairs of beady eyes. He was still trapped him in the nightmare. His mom waking him up was just another sick game to this woman that brought him here.

Zion screamed, sobbing as once again his nightmare shifted. He was now running for his life through the halls of his old school. The spider scuttled hurriedly on the ceiling, trying to slash at him with her barbed front legs.

"HELP! SOMEBODY HELP ME!" Zion's voice bounced off the walls of the empty school.

He looked back over his shoulder to see her still pursing him. His legs were growing heavier the longer he ran. He had to keep going or he would die and then it would start over again. Desperately, Zion tried to open one of the locked doors down the hall. None of them were open.

A light flicking on further down the hall drew his attention. Pumping his legs as hard as he could, Zion raced towards the lit room. Behind him, his mother, the spider, screeched. Her prey was getting away. Lifting her body, she shot webs at him, trying to snare him, to slow him down.

Zion was almost to the room. If he could just make it there, he knew he would be safe. The room was barely a few pumps of his feet away when a thin thread of web caught his shoulder. Screeching, his mom reared up, using her front legs to pull him and the web back towards her.

Clawing for anything to grab onto, Zion tried to reach for the door handle to pull himself forward. His hand missed, and he grabbed air. This was it; he was going to die again. Maybe this time he wouldn't come back. Why didn't anyone come to save him? His hand fell away from the handle as he was drug backwards. A small, dainty hand grabbed hold of his.

Zion looked up, afraid some new terror joined in torturing him. He looked up into eyes whiter than snow. Her hold on him was strong and warm. With extreme effort, she pulled Zion into the room and slammed the door shut. The terrifying screeches of his mother, furious as he had gotten away, rang through the hall. Terrified she was going to come charging through the door, Zion backed away from the door, looking for an escape.

The small woman turned to watch him as he tried to find a way out. "It's ok she won't find you here." The soft voice spoke hoping to soothe him. Her words had the opposite effect. He seemed more frantic to get free. Wanting to calm him, she stepped closer. That was a mistake. Zion practically tried to claw up the wall to get further away from her.

Holding her hands up, she backed away from him and sat down on the floor in-front of him. "It's ok," she said again in that same calming tone. " I won't come any closer."

Still weary of her intentions, Zion calmed down a degree when a few seconds went by and she kept her word, staying in the same spot. He watched her closely, waiting for her to kill or change into some gigantic monster.

"Are — you — going to eat me?" he fearfully questioned. The tiny woman cocked her head to the side at his strange question. "Why would I eat you? From where I'm sitting you wouldn't be much of a meal." her reply intended as a joke put him back on edge. Sighing, she changed the subject, hoping to distract him.

"What's your name?" she asked. "My name is Nike," the woman said when the silence stretched on, and her question was unanswered.

He stared at her, confused. None of the other monsters had talked or asked him what his name was. This could be some new trick created by this horrible nightmare.

Still suspicious of her, Zion scooted further away just in case she was lying and changed into a flesh-eating monster. His body hurt all over from running and the deaths they brought him back from. Nike could see he was exhausted. He wouldn't be able to endure much more. His mind was on the verge of breaking.

"Do you want this nightmare to stop?" Nike spoke softly to him.

Zion tensed. He had nowhere to run to. She was sitting in front of the only way out. There were no windows in the classroom for him to get through.

Annoyed, Nike repeated her question. " Do you want this nightmare to stop?" Outside the door, Zion heard the sickening screech of his mother — the spider. Something heavy slammed against the door, denting it inwards. A disgustingly sweet order filled the room. One long barbed leg stabbed blindly. Nike braced herself against the door. Somehow, she kept the door from breaking as his mother's body slammed into it repeatedly.

Raising a hand while still bracing the door, Nike sent a powerful blast towards Zion, hoping she didn't kill him, they were out of options. If he didn't wake up now, he would really die this time.

ZION LAUNCHED HIMSELF out of the chair, avoiding the blast he thought was coming for him. His movement startled his mother awake.

"WHAT IS WRONG WITH YOU!!!" she screamed at him.

He backed quickly away from her, putting the raggedy old chair between them for protection. Michelle glared angrily at her son. Still tired from driving so far and only sleeping for a few scant hours, she was not in the mood for whatever game he was playing.

"Explain yourself!" his mother yelled at him, pushing the chair out of the way.

Not knowing what to say Zion, went with the first thing that came to mind. "I want to go home." he said in a quiet voice.

Michelle stared incredulously at her son. He wanted to go home, so that was his excuse for waking her up after she had driven for so long. There was no way this was for real. He had to be joking with her.

"YOU WOKE ME UP BECAUSE YOU WANT TO GO HOME?" Michelle spat at him.

Lowering his head to hide the tears, he knew would only upset her more. Zion nodded. Why was his mother so angry with him? He just wanted her to hold him and love him like she used to.

He was never afraid of his mom, but now Zion stood in the corner cowering from the only family he had left. His dad's death didn't seem to bother her at all.

"Mom, do you even care that dad is dead?" Zion choked out, sobbing.

Michelle stared, perplexed. What was he talking about? Patrick wasn't dead. She may not have known where he was currently, but he wasn't dead.

"Zion you're being ridiculous. Your father isn't dead. He is somewhere getting high like he usually does." She said, shaking her head.

"I SAW HIM! HE WAS DEAD ON OUR COUCH — AND THEN HE JUST VANISHED!" Zion bellowed. He couldn't control himself anymore. He was afraid, his body hurt, and his mom was acting crazy.

Heat flooded Michelle's caramel cheeks. She did not appreciate being yelled at by her eleven-year-old.

"DON'T RAISE YOUR VOICE TO ME! I AM YOUR MOTHER! I HAVE PUT UP WITH YOUR ATTITUDE SINCE YOUR FATHER LEFT US. I WILL NOT HAVE YOU

DISRESPCTING ME WHEN I'M NOT THE ONE WHO DIDN''T WANT YOU!"

The words were out of her mouth before she could stop them. Breathing heavily, Michelle grabbed her purse and keys, slamming the door to the hotel behind her. She needed to get away from Zion before she did something irrational.

Zion heard his mother's car start and speed away. He wanted to run after her, his legs wouldn't move. Over and over, he heard his mother say nobody wanted him. Zion slammed his fist into the wall.

This wasn't fair. He had done nothing wrong. Yesterday was his birthday, he didn't even get to celebrate. Still not satisfied, Zion yanked the phone out of the wall, throwing it across the room. He tore through the room, throwing and breaking anything, he could get his hands on. Still, it did nothing to fix the hole he felt in his heart.

FRACTURED BONDS

Michelle drove, not knowing where she was going. she just had to get away from Zion. Being around him made her want to hurt him. Every time she looked into his hazel eyes; it was Patrick she saw.

Angry tears flowed down her face as she kept driving aimlessly. Patrick was supposed to be the love of her life. He left her so easily, without a second thought. Not only that, but he also left her to raise their son.

Now that she was up and moving, her body yelled that she needed to eat. Pulling into the only place that was open at five in the morning. Michelle parked and headed into the diner.

"Welcome, make yourself comfortable and I'll be right, witcha. "A woman's voice called from behind the counter. Michelle debated siting at the counter before changing her mind and choosing a small booth towards the back facing the door.

She couldn't shake the feeling of unease that had crept over her while she drove away from the hotel. Zion's words echoing in her head. There was no way Patrick was dead. She remembered seeing him leave days before Zi's birthday.

The painful memory resurfacing caused her to flinch. Patrick had been beside himself trying to find money for his next fix. She had come home to him, tearing the house apart, looking for the money she had hidden. She had taken to hiding money so they wouldn't fall behind on bills, with him spending everything to feed his addiction. When he hadn't found the money, Patrick turned on her, getting aggressive.

Michelle remembered feeling his hands on her throat as he sat on her chest, screaming for her to tell him where the money was. He released her long enough to rustle through her purse, snagging the last few dollars she had. How could Zi not understand how much she had suffered staying with his father so long?

Michelle had done her best to keep Patrick's abusive behavior from Zi. That day, he had seen firsthand what his father was capable of. When Patrick had come back that night, he was angry and high. His clothes reeked of urine and metal. He had bloodshot eyes and dirty hair. He tried to come onto her, but Michelle wasn't having it that night. She pushed him off her, only to have him slap hard across the face before continuing to remove her underwear. Her repeated screams of no brought Zion out of his room.

Her sweet baby boy rushed his father to protect her. Patrick was stronger than he was. Watching Patrick beat their son had been the last straw.

She had to move them away where Patrick wouldn't be able to hurt them. Part of her wondered how Zi didn't remember that. Where was the sweet boy that rushed in to save her from his abusive father? Instead, now all she saw was an angry pre-teen. Anger directed at her for making them move. Sure, she was a little frustrated with Zion. He just needed to toughen up. The waitress approaching with a menu in hand drew Michelle away from the painful past clouding her mind.

"Hi, I'm Shelia. Can I getcha any thang ta drink ta start ya off with?" the older woman greeted her with a thick southern accent. "Hun are you ok?"

Ordering a coffee and two pancakes, Michelle passed the menu back to Shelia, ignoring her question. The woman seemed friendly, but Michelle just wanted to sit in her booth undisturbed. She just needed time to process the emotions washing over her. Closing her eyes, Michelle braced her head on the table. A soft hand gently shook her awake. It felt like only seconds had passed. Lifting her head, Michelle noticed the time on her phone. For three hours she had slept in the diner.

The sun now shone through the windows, briefly blinding her. She must have been more tired than she realized. Several missed calls from a number she didn't recognize flashed on her phone. Michelle looked up, expecting to see the same friendly older woman that had taken her order. She stared into the face of a much younger waitress.

"Umm Sorry Miss, you can't sleep here." The young waitress said.

Embarrassed, Michelle gathered her things, leaving money on the table to cover her untouched meal. Her phone rang just as she got back in her car to drive back to the hotel.

"Hello. Michelle?" A deep male voice questioned through her car's speakers.

"Hello?" Michelle answered back, unsure who could call her so early.

"Hi. umm, this is David Pittman Ma'am. The uh paramedic from the other day?" He chuckled into the phone.

Michelle didn't know why. Hearing his name had her heart beating faster and her cheeks blushing.

"Oh yes. David, um, how can I help you?" she said nervously, brushing her hair behind her ears as if he could see her.

There was a long pause before David spoke again. "I'm sorry I stopped by your house to check on you and Zion. it seemed no one was there."

Michelle blushed. She didn't think it was weird at all. It was sweet that he wanted to check up on her. She wondered how he had gotten her number. She didn't remember giving it. About to say as much, David cut her off before she could get the question out.

"I hope you don't think I'm some sort of creep or anything. I pulled your number off the dispatch report because I was worried."

Michelle smiled to herself; it had been a while since any man had shown so much concern for her. Patrick stopped caring about her the second he found his new love for drugs.

She wanted his attention, wanted to feel attractive to someone. And David made her feel desired and beautiful. All he had done was his job. She felt drawn to him. Her body wanted him. She could feel her body respond to his voice alone.

The desire to feel his body up against hers, and let him have his way with her, flooded through her. Michelle remembered feeling this excitement when she first married Patrick. The heat flooding through her body now differed from before. David made her feel safe. And he sparked a fire in her that Patrick never had. She missed feeling secure and wanted.

The overwhelming weight of everything came rushing back, and Michelle couldn't control herself. She broke down crying. Her loud sobs echoed over the speaker, alarming David.

"Michelle, what's wrong? Are you ok?" the concern in his voice made her cry even harder. He was a stranger, and he seemed to care more for her than her own husband and son.

She had been gone for hours, and Zion hadn't even called to check on her. Did he even care that she wasn't back yet? He was just like Patrick, only thinking about himself and what she could do for them. Pulling herself together, Michelle explained everything that had happened with Patrick and her decision to leave South Carolina. David sat and listened to everything she had to say without interrupting. Michelle worried his silence meant he was going to regret calling her. That was the last thing she wanted to happen. David was her only lifeline right now. She didn't think she could handle losing someone so valuable. When he finally spoke, his voice was calm and understanding.

"I'm sorry you've been carrying so much by yourself. This may not be my place, if your husband isn't willing to seek help." He paused before continuing, "Then he isn't worth your time. You're far too beautiful to be worrying about a man that doesn't want to give you the world."

That left her breathless. Was David saying he wanted to give her the world? Or was he just saying that to sound as if he cared about her?

Michelle didn't want to be that gullible woman that fell for every nice thing a man said.

"Thank you, David, that was very sweet of you to say. And thank you for caring enough to check on up me. I must get back to Zion. I've been gone for a long time."

David fell silent, debating what to say next. Or at least Michelle hoped that's why he was being so quiet. She was afraid he had taken her thanks for a rude dismissal. She just couldn't entertain thoughts of another man until she settled everything with Patrick.

"Tell you what, you call me when you're done playing house with that piece of trash." David said angrily before hanging up.

His cold change in attitude threw her off. Had she upset him? Now she felt bad. Maybe she should call him back to apologize. Before she could hit the redial button, her phone rang with another number. She didn't know.

"Hello?" she answered uncertainly.

"Hello Miss, we received several noise complaints from the rooms surrounding yours."

"Ma'am, I must remind you we will bill directly any damage done to the room to you. And if the noise continues, we will ask you to vacate the building."

Michelle hung the phone after reassuring the manager that she would try to keep the noise down from now on. She didn't know what Zion had been up to. Heading back to the hotel, she intended to find out immediately.

ZION SAT IN THE CORNER of the trashed hotel room. His knees drawn up to his chest. Angry tears dripped onto the legs of his pants. He had broken everything he could in the room. None of it helped to calm his anger. There was now a hollowness inside him since his mom left the hotel. He would have broken more in the room. He was tired and didn't have the energy to keep going. For the tenth time Zion's stomach growled, reminding him that his mother had denied getting him any food the nine-hour drive from South Carolina. The hotel door swung open, banging off the wall.

His mother stood in the doorway, growing angrier as she took in the damage he had done to the room. Zion opened his mouth to apologize, stopped. No, this was her fault. He didn't want to be here. Zion met his mother's furious stare with defiance. If she wanted to hate him, then fine.

The room was a mess. No wonder the hotel staff called her. He must have made a lot of noise, tearing the room apart. There was no way they were going to stay here after tonight. She was too tired to think about that right now.

Walking past Zion and the mess, Michelle went straight to the bathroom to shower. She would figure something out after she slept more. Zion waited for his mother to scream and yell at him. She said nothing after her shower. She laid back down to sleep without a glance in his direction.

Ignoring the pain in his stomach Zion, stretched out on the filthy floor. Falling asleep as soon as his head touched the floor. He jerked awake to the sound of scratching. Looking around, he expected to see a spider scuttling towards him. He saw nothing moving towards him on the royal blue rug with gold trim he was lying on.

Except he didn't remember the hotel room having a fancy rug.

UNRAVELED PATHS

Tentatively, Zion stood up, looking around the unfamiliar room. He stood in a wide stone built room. Sunlight flooded the room from the large open glass windows leading to the balcony. On an enormous bed in the center of the room sat Gaea, the green-haired woman, writing peacefully in what he assumed was a journal. She seemed older than before, yet still held a youthful, radiant air.

"Hello" Zion said tentatively. The woman sitting on the bed writing gave no sign she heard him. He waved his arms around and she kept writing as if he wasn't there.

She radiated with a decadent beauty. Her wild, untamed green hair flowed freely down her back. She was petite and delicate, like a flower. Soft amber skin glowed as the sun touched it. Was this real? Zion hesitantly stepped closer. If he was still dreaming, he shouldn't be able to touch her, right? His hand was inches away.

"WHERE IS HE?" King Euthydemus' voice roared barging into Gaea's room unannounced. The abrupt roar of the man's voice made him jump back a few steps. Afraid of being caught in the room, Zion rushed to hide. The King walked right through him as if he wasn't even there. His skin grey translucent a distant memory of from the past.

Gaea slowly raised her Harlequin- green eyes, returning his angry stare with nonchalance. She had grown used to him busting into her room unexpectedly. He had taken to doing this more frequently after he allowed Uranis to stay in recent years.

She didn't understand his jealously of Uranis. He wanted nothing to do with any of them, and he mostly kept to himself. He even ignored her most days. Choosing to fly above the castle during the day and train to fight at night.

Sighing, she rose to her feet, ignoring Euthydemus' outrage. Calmly, she walked to the balcony. Her eyes quickly locating the golden eagle flying above the treetops. Wetting her lips, she whistled loudly. Letting out a loud screech, he answered her call. Tilting his wings and angling back towards her. The wind from his wings grabbed at her clothes, whipping it around her body. As he drew closer, Zion could see how large he really was. Hovering just outside the window, he was easily as tall as three men standing on each other's shoulders. A large giant yellow eye stared pointedly in the room. For the briefest second, landing on Zion. Had he seen him or had Zion only imagined?

Before their eyes, the golden eagle transformed into a youthful boy of nine~ and ~ ten. Skye blue hair grazed his broad shoulders and ancient static-blue eyes swept over the King and his guards standing in her room. He had changed a lot since Zion had last dreamt about him. Every aspect of his physique stretched to unprecedented proportions. His long legs extending like pillars granted him an imposing verticality that seemed to touch the heavens. Arms the size of tree trunks hung by his side. Anyone with a brain would have known to avoid him. King Euthydemus continued to glare angrily at Uranis.

Their first year together Uranis wouldn't leave her side. He clung to her like she was his lifeline. She resented him for it at first, but she started feeling empty when he wasn't around. Being around Uranis felt like being close to the sun. Shifting her thoughts from the boy he was to the man standing in front of her. She couldn't help but feel dwarfed, both literally and metaphorically. His presence was powerful and demanding. If she didn't know any better, she would have sworn they all should bow to him.

"Giatí me káleses? *-Why did you call me?"* he spoke in a musical language only Gaea and Zion could understand.

"The king and I worried you were not OK," Gaea responded so Euthydemus could understand.

Uranis understood her. He refused to use the language the king spoke. Gaea suspected he did this just to irritate Euthydemus.

Zion watched from the corner of the room, not saying a word. He wondered would they hear him if he spoke?

"YOU DO NOT HAVE MY PERMISSION TO LEAVE THE GROUNDS!" Euthydemus raged, as his alabaster skin turned a nasty shade of red.

Gaea turned addressing Euthydemus, "He didn't leave the grounds. He was just above them." The king flustered turning even redder. A thick vein throbbed viciously on his temple. Uranis leveled a bored glance in the king's direction. Before shifting his eyes back to Gaea.

"Giatí chreiázomai tin ádeiá sas gia na káno otidípote anthrópini vromiá? *—Why do I need your permission to do anything human filth?"* He spoke directly to Gaea, dismissing Euthydemus altogether.

Uranis turned to leave, back out the window. He had no wish to be cooped up in the stone prison. Though he accepted Gaea was used to the cage they kept her in. But he refused to be caged by anyone ever again. Focused on shifting his body back to the golden eagle. He didn't notice Euthydemus rushing at his back, dagger in hand. Zion opened his mouth to warn Uranis, forgetting that no one could see or hear him.

Euthydemus was almost to Uranis when a vine grabbed his wrist. The tip of the blade stopping a breath away from his spine. Yet again, he had foolishly let his guard down. Lowering his shoulders, he stalked towards Euthydemus with slowly determined strides.

A raised hand from Gaea stopping his advance. She no longer wore the warm, gentle glow Zion had seen on her before. It scared him to see her face contorted with anger. The room flooded with a sinister green light pouring out of her.

"What — What — Are, You Doing?" Euthydemus spoke as the vine wrapped around his thick neck. His head turned a dangerous shade of blue. The vine tightened restricting his airway.

Rushing forward, the guards attempted to subdue her. A gust of wind ripped through the room. Slicing them in half before they could reach her. Her voice was soft as she spoke. But there was no mistaking the tremor running down her body.

"You tried to kill him. He's done nothing to you," Gaea cried, raising her head to meet his gaze. She hoped he would apologize and show some remorse. But in his eyes, he was unrepentant. He would do it again.

"YOU ARE MINE!!" Euthydemus choked out.

Her vision darkened; her eyes flashed dangerously. **Non sum, Mater omnis creationis. Sum Dea Gaea et nulli homini pertineo! —** *No, I AM THE MOTHER OF ALL CREATION. I AM THE GODDESS GAEA! I BELONG TO NO MAN!*"

The vines around his wrist and ankles pulled in opposite directions. Stretching his limbs in impossible angles. His horrified screams shattered the quiet. Blood spilled out of his torso. Throughout the room, the metallic smell with a cold, detached expression, Gaea watched as it ripped him apart. The royal blue carpet drunk in his blood like a starving animal. The crimson stain turning the once elegant rug into sopping wet pool.

Zion watched, horrified. His stomach turning looking at the pieces of the king laying in front of him. She killed him so easily. Gaea's cold, unyielding gaze remained fixed on Euthydemus. The room held its breath, and with a sickening finality, the vines achieved their grisly purpose. Euthydemus's form lay shattered, a gruesome mosaic of the once-powerful king.

When the last breath escaped Euthydemus' lips the marks on Gaea and Uranis scolded their skin. Zion screamed as fire exploded down his back. Burning a pattern into his back. In different parts of Greece, men and women screamed out as they too were marked. Tattoos like Gaea's etched onto their skin. Zion heard their collective screams of pain. Their confusion and fear overwhelmed him.

Uranis struggled to his feet, crawling over the lifeless pieces of Euthydemus.

"Quid fit? Quis sunt hi homines — *What is happening? Who are these people?"* He asked, stepping closer to Gaea.

"Sunt liberi nostri. — *They are our children."* She said in awe.

Behind her, the frenzied steps and clang of metal reached their ears. Pulling her towards the balcony, Uranis transformed into the golden eagle. Gaea scrambled onto his back. Just as more guards burst into her room. He spread his massive wings, stretching roughly twenty-three meters. With several quick flaps they soared over the outer wall of the estate. Zion stood on the balcony, watching them disappear above the clouds.

"WHAT ARE YOU STARING at?" a soft feminine voice whispered close to his ear. Startling him enough, he almost fell over the banister. Zion turned to see Nike, the girl that almost killed him in his nightmare. Afraid she was back to finish him, Zion glanced around nervously for a weapon. She stood, blocking his way to the nearest object.

"Wait, you can see me?" He questioned.

Nike cocked her head to the side, silver strands of hair falling across her eyes, confused by his question. Course she could see him. He was standing right next to her.

"Am I not supposed to see you? Oh, are you playing that human game hide-and-seek?" She answered excitedly. "I'm good at that game. Well, I'm good at all games, really."

Zion said nothing, his eyes continued to dart around the room for an escape. He could probably shove past her. She didn't look all that strong. Rushing towards her, he changed directions at the last second, bolting towards the open door.

"Why are you running?" Nike said, appearing a few feet in front of him. Zion fell back, startled by her sudden appearance, causing him to lose balance. He stared at her mouth open in shock. Seconds ago, she was standing on the balcony. Now she stood, blocking his only exit.

People didn't just vanish and reappear out of thin air or change into giant birds. He must have lost his mind. Yeah, that was it. He was going crazy. He just needed to find some food, and everything would go back to normal.

Getting up, Zion ignored the teenage looking girl with silver hair. He walked past her, determined to find something to eat to feed his loud stomach. Nike turned as he brushed past her. His long gangly arms swinging to a rhythm only he could hear. He was a strange human. The first time they met, he accused her of wanting to eat him.

Though she wanted to eat him, just not in the way he thought. Following close behind him, Nike took in their surroundings. Most humans dreamed about their own lives or past lovers. It intrigued her that Zion was dreaming about an old castle.

Behind him, the soft footsteps continued following him. She would go away once he found food. He navigated the halls of the castle with ease. Trying random doors to see where they led. Every door he tried remained locked. The hallways and doors blended. He could no longer tell them apart.

Nike watched Zion closely keep back a respectful distance between them. As he grew more frantic with each door that wouldn't open. Concerned, he would turn that anger towards her. She had seen it before. Humans always lashed out at others when they didn't get their way.

She'd seen the nastiness inside each one of them, no matter the age. Men who attacked women for their own pleasure. Girls humiliating other girls out of fear of being abandoned by friends. Zion would be no different, he would attack her too.

She followed him to the kitchen. It was empty except for a bowl of untouched fruit.

"Have you been here before?" she asked.

"No," Zion said simply, without turning.

"Then how did you know where the kitchen was?" she asked.

Zion shrugged as he continued his search for something other than the fruit sitting in the bowl. He hadn't really thought about how he knew; he had just followed his instincts. Finding nothing else worth eating, Zion grabbed a red apple. His mouth watering, he took the biggest bite his mouth would allow.

The apple in his mouth tasted different. His mouth felt dry as he continued to chew but, he couldn't taste anything. Thinking the apple has just gone bad, Zion spit the apple out and grabbed another fruit from the bowl. Taking a bite, he tasted nothing. Grabbing a handful of grapes, he popped several in his mouth. There was no flavor.

"You're strange, human." Nike said, with her head cocked to one side. "Are all humans slow minded?"

Now Zion was confused. Why did she say human like she wasn't one?

"Those aren't real apples," Nike said simply.

Zion didn't know what she meant. Of course, they were real. They were all just spoiled from sitting for so long. Pushing the fruit aside, Zion headed towards the door, intending to leave and head back to the hotel.

He tugged on the door several times, and it didn't budge. Bracing his foot, Zion pulled with all his might, but the door refused to open.

"That door won't open," Nike said, swinging her feet as she sat at the table, watching him struggle.

"What do you know? You're not even real," Zion said over his shoulder.

Confused, Nike raised her hand, examining it in the light. That was an odd thing to say. She felt real. The blood pumping in her veins was real.

Zion kept pulling at the door. He was growing desperate, and his aching stomach wasn't helping.

"Ugh, why isn't this stupid door opening?" Zion said, tugging in frustration.

When tugging didn't work, Zion kicked the door repeatedly. Nike sat watching him, content to sit quietly until he grew tired of hurting himself. Humans always wanted to do things the hard way.

He kicked the door several more times. His emotions getting the better of him, Zion threw his whole body into the door. He felt caged and trapped, like an animal.

"I WANT OUT! LET ME OUT!" Zion roared before punching the door, tears streaming down his face. He just wanted to go home. Why couldn't he leave?

Nike glanced at him, curious about his outburst. For a second, his voice had changed, and she felt traces of Zeus raising within him. Jumping off the table, slowly she walked towards the boy as he continued to strike the door. Her heart wept for him. The life ahead of him was going to be rough. She wished she could undo what Hecate had set in motion. But she did not have power over fate. Not familiar with the emotions of humans. She did the only thing that came naturally to her. Wrapping her arms around his trembling body.

Gently pulling him away from the door. He clung to her body and wept. She saw him not as the vessel he had become, but the boy whose mother let her own grief turn her against him.

His mother should have protected and loved him. Instead, she succumbed to the hatred Hecate had fed into her heart. Nike sat with her arms around him until his sobs grew silent.

DIVINE AWAKENING

In the solemn expanse of the Congressional Medal of Honor Memorial, Zion stood, overlooking the empty Canal. The pungent scent of fish and murky water assaulted his senses. The night was quiet, a stark contrast to the usual crowded scene during his nightly walks along the three-mile stretch. An eerie stillness hung in the air; lightning silently lite up the night. Hinting at the storm clawing like a caged tiger desperate for its release. Everyone with any sense had stayed safely indoors. Zion squinted against the gusts of wind, his eyes eventually finding a bit of peace in that mural on the canal walls he knew so well. The two dragons, facing each other and that blue sun made of glass - he'd studied every detail of that thing more times than he could count. The way the glass pieces caught the sunlight, scattering it across the grimy walkway and the rank water, it was burned into his brain.

Those dragons, they were like the war raging inside him every damn day. Eight years of his stepdad David wailing on him, beating him down in every way possible... Zion was tired, man. Tired deep in his bones. But those dragons, they represented the fight still left in him, even if it was buried under pain and exhaustion.

He couldn't help but feel a connection to that mural. The artist got it - life could be brutal, with forces battering you from all sides. But you couldn't let it break you. No matter how weary he felt, no matter how much he wanted to give up sometimes, Zion knew he had to keep fighting. Maybe not with fists, but by staying strong inside, not letting

David destroy who he was. Those dragons reminded him of that. They gave him just a tiny bit of hope to hang on to.

Tonight, David's drunken rage had driven him here to mural. But even as he tried to focus on the dragons, the memories of that one night kept clawing their way to the surface. It was like a twisted movie playing out on the murky water of the canal, every painful detail as vivid as the day it happened. Zion couldn't escape it, couldn't push it back down no matter how hard he tried.

That night, when David's rage had reached a terrifying peak, had left scars on Zion's mind that were just as real as the ones on his body. The fear, the pain, the helplessness - they were all right there, threatening to drag him under. But something about the mural, about those dragons locked in their eternal battle, gave Zion a flicker of strength.

THE MEMORY OF THAT horrible night, November 10, 2010, slammed into Zion like a freight train as he stood there by the canal, the storm raging around him. He was back in that living room, watching helplessly as his world shattered into a million bloody pieces.

His mom's words echoed in his head, that simple question that had set off a chain reaction of violence and chaos. "David, what are you doing?" She had no idea what she was unleashing when she confronted that monster.

Zion could still see it all playing out, like a sick, twisted movie. One he couldn't look away from or run from. David's rage, boiling over until it consumed everything in its path. His mom, standing tall and brave even as David came at her with all his brutality. And Zion, throwing himself into the middle of it all, desperate to protect the only person who'd ever really loved him.

But David, he was too strong, too vicious. Zion felt the impact of his body hitting the wall, heard the crack of bone and the rush of blood in his ears. And then David's voice, cutting through the pain and confusion like a jagged blade.

"YOU THINK YOU'RE BETTER THAN ME? YOU'RE NOTHING!"

Those words, like poison, seeped into Zion's veins and rotting him from the inside out. Because the truth was, he did think he was better than David. Better than the violence and the abuse and the endless cycle of pain.

But in that moment, lying there on the floor with his head spinning and his body aching, Zion felt lower than he ever had before. And then he saw his mom, crumpled and motionless, with David standing over her

AS THE WOMAN'S SCREAM pierced the air, his attention was drawn to the opposite bank of the canal, where three figures grappled with small figure. Her auburn hair flowed like the leaves of autumn, as she desperately tried to protect herself from the men closing in on her.

Zion's gaze fell upon the blond holding her, his wealth evident in his demeanor. His golden hair, slicked back, exuded an air of arrogance. The flash of crimson hair trailed behind a tall muscular man who gave off a rockstar vibe. The third, shrouded in shadows, reminded Zion of the grim reaper, sending a chill down his spine. Laughter rang out shattering the cold unyielding grip that had seized him. Warmth spread back through his body, dispelling the stiffness that had settled in his bones. He watched in disbelief as the violence unfolded before him. She broke free from of her captors and turned to stare directly at him. Her lavender eyes, speckled with a chaotic swirl of blue and red, burned with an intensity that pierced him to the depths of his soul. The scent of juniper and lavender drifted through the air, a stark contrast to the harsh stench of the canal.

He stood frozen, his mind racing and his body itching to move, his instincts screaming for him to help her. She needed a hero, someone like one of the many names that littered the wall behind him. Someone that wasn't him. Heroes didn't let their stepdads beat on them. A hero would have saved his mom instead of crying. Gritting his teeth Zion turned to walk away. "Zion, I need your help. I can't do this alone," the soft whisper forced him to stop. All movement stopped as the heavy stares of all three men bore into him, awaiting his response. The only audible sound was the loud thrumming in his ears as he met their gazes, his own eyes heating up. Suppressing the rising anger within him, Zion turned away from all of them. This wasn't his fight. There was nothing ...HE ... could do.

"Please don't leave me," she implored, her voice a fragile plea that tugged at him. Yet, he kept walking, distancing himself from whatever was about to happen. The sound of a heavy hand slapping flesh echoed behind him. The same instant the air crackled with energy, and the wind slammed the water against the canal bank. Nature itself was furious by the violence against her. Crossing the bridge without even thinking, Zion found himself face to face with the muscled rockstar. His feet carrying him forward as his mind screamed at him to turn back. He approached Zion, with an arrogant swagger that radiated from every pore. His fist clenched; Zion slugged him. A blow that should have wiped the smug grin off his overly handsome face. But he mockingly laughed as if the blow was a soft kiss. His eyes glinted with sadistic amusement. Too late Zion realized that he was in over his head. Every instinct he had warned him to run.

"You've got guts, kid, but you'll need more that," the man taunted, laughter echoing from stupid drones behind him.

Zion charged forward his body overflowing with an unearthly power. His eyes sparked with traces of lightning, accompanied by the deafening sound of thunder booming. The laugher dying almost immediately, their attention fixed on the canal that had transformed into a battleground of the elements. The wind and rain whipped around him, plastering his clothes to his body, but he ignored it and the chaos going on around him. His, rage boiled over pushing every other thought out of his mind. He wanted to break the large man standing before him. Wanted it badly enough that he could taste it.

Too focused on the man with crimson hair, Zion missed the sudden blur that knocked him off his feet. Moving with a speed that defied the laws of nature grim reaper reject slugged him again. A thunderous impact reverberated through Zion's jaw as his fist connected with brutal force. Blood spewed from his mouth, the metallic taste of copper and salt filling his mouth. Several teeth fell from his mouth hitting the pavement.

Despite the searing pain, Zion glared at the blue-haired assailant, masking his suffering with a defiant laugh. "Is that all you got?" he taunted. That was a mistake unanimously they attacked him as one.

He had to give them credit. His stepdad's beatings paled in comparison to the merciless assault he now endured. The irony that he would miss David's abuse made him laugh. The unfairness of it all. Was there ever a moment when he wasn't being beat? Their blows sent ripples through his organs as they battered him relentlessly. Each strike cruel and unforgiving as his torment continued. He kicked the legs of the tallest man. Steeling himself he managed to rise to his feet. Squaring his shoulders Zion glared at each of them through swollen slits. And did the dumbest thing he knew how to do. He quoted the only phrase he could think of. "To infinity and beyond bitches!" Overhead, lightning crackled, casting an eerie glow on the walls of the canal.

A bolt hurtled towards him; a resigned sigh escaped his lips. Death seemed imminent, promising an end to the unrelenting cycle of abuse.

The lightning exploded onto the canal, throwing them against the museum wall. Instead of delivering the expected demise, he had hoped. Energy surged into Zion making him feel more alive. The agony subsided, replaced by an overwhelming sense of vitality.

Reality slowed down around him, the collision of heat and ions, lighting up the entire area. The storm's raw power unfolded before him. A newfound hunger for a primal force surged within him. In the back of his mind crackling intensified growing louder until it sounded like it came from every direction.

A commanding voice echoed, urging him to unleash the dormant power.

"Free me, boy! you, will have all the power you need."

The voice, laced with agitation, pressed upon his consciousness. Yet, the mysterious guidance remained unnoticed by the others. The malevolent storm and the echoing voice mingled.

"Boy, what are you waiting for?" The voice thundered; a tempest of urgency echoed through Zion's mind. He winced at the sheer intensity. The commanding tone rubbed him the wrong way. Who did they or it think he was? But it wasn't just a voice; it was a force that demanded his attention.

Shaking his head, Zion attempted to dismiss the unsettling presence within him. Perhaps he had taken one too many to the head. "Pull yourself together, Zion," he muttered, fighting the intrusion into his thoughts.

Glancing at the once-menacing trio, now frozen in eerie stillness, Zion waved his hand toward the crimson-haired figure. No reaction. The world itself seemed to have hit the pause button. leaves hung in mid-air; the wind held its breath. Zion bewildered, plucked a leaf out of the air.

An inexplicable force held everything in place. It was unsettling how calm everything was even though it was just storming moments ago. "How is this possible?" Zion questioned the silence, the leaf crumbled but the pieces refused to fall.

The voice persisted, mocking his confusion. "How much longer will you play with leaves, boy?"

"You're not the boss of me!" he silently challenged the unseen presence, his defiance unmistakable. In a sudden flash, he found himself transported to a grand, opulent hall. Beyond a colossal archway, the distant rumble of thunder echoed, and the faint flashes of lightning danced across the distant sky.

Blue eyes peered through the arch, and the voice commanded, "Open the door, boy."

Perplexed, Zion hesitated. Why should he listen? As if it could read his thoughts, a tempest hurled him against the wall. Dazed and confused he slowly stood back up to face the unseen force.

"What do I have to do then?" he implored, facing the unyielding silence.

The voice finally spoke cryptically, "Before you open a door, you must be willing to walk through, boy." One thick eyebrow rose in confusion. What did that even mean?

Understanding finally dawned on him, he spoke with confidence. The words presenting themselves to him as if he had spoken to them a thousand times. **"Te accipio et omnem tuam fortitudinem. Corpus meum offero ut vas vivens pro Iove, Domino Caeli et Rege Olympii."** — *I accept you and all your strength. – I offer my body as a living vessel for Zeus, the Lord of Heaven, and the King of Olympus.*

The barrier shattered, and Zion was back on the canal, the trio unfrozen. They vanished, seconds before a colossal lightning bolt came streaking down. Zion planted his feet firmly and braced himself for the pain. Knowledge flowed into him—languages, glimpses of lives past and future. Within him he felt the minds of others. His body convulsed, discharging power that damaging the surroundings. Visions of countless deaths flashed in his mind. Gritting his teeth, he pulled Zeus' power, into himself. Just as quickly as it had come the storm subsided, leaving the canal an unnatural hush. Exhausted, Zion passed out, a smile on his face. He had done it.

"HOW IS HE NOT DEAD?" Ares, the god of war questioned materializing beside Zion motionless body. Hera, queen of the gods, and the two other men reappeared, their eyes wide with disbelief.

"I'm still unsure." she replied.

She bent down, attempting to gently brush away the blood from his face. However, the sparks dancing on his skin seared her fingertips. Hera scrutinized the mortal before her. Within him stirred the power of her husband, yet he was not under Zeus' control. She detested the manipulation that had altered his life, but for the sake of protecting her family, she was willing to go to any lengths.

As she continued to gaze down at Zion, a twinge of sorrow gripped her heart. The memory of him growing up amidst pain and indifference brought a deep sadness to her lavender eyes. Now, he was burdened with the power of an Olympian King. He would have to carry a weight that fate had thrust upon him. Tapping into her divine abilities Hera, sought to glimpse his future.

Briefly, she saw him seated on a golden throne atop Olympus. The fleeting vision left her before she could see further. Frustrated, her powers were abruptly cut off. Someone was blocking her. That unsettled her there were few powers that could trump her own. Whoever possessed such capabilities posed a threat to her and the other Olympians.

"Hera, what have you done? This human," Hades, spat the word with disgust. "Now has more power than all of us."

Lifting her chaotic gaze, she fixed him with an icy stare freezing the air around them. Her voice quivered with rage.

"Hades, remember your place when addressing me."

His eyes darkened, the shadows stretched like obsidian tendrils. Their combined powers crackled and sizzled, sending waves of heat through the tense atmosphere.

"Mother, I'm sure Uncle meant no disrespect. Though I am curious how a mortal is able to possess enough willpower to suppress a god." Apollo, the God of the sun, interrupted the stand-off between them.

Reigning in their powers, the two gods glared daggers at each other.

"We must reclaim Zeus' power before he fully bonds with them permanently," Apollo continued.

Ares wet his lips with eagerness. He raised his hand, summoning a ball of pure, godly energy. Apollo, opened his mouth attempting to warn his brother before he unleashed the power

"Ares, that won't work on him,"

Disregarding the warning, Ares a smug grin etched on his face, he unleashed the blast. The forceful recoil sent him hurtling backward, into the wall with a resounding smack, leaving behind a sizable crack. Golden blood-ichor poured from a cavity in his chest.

The potency of the blast would have annihilated him had he not hastily shielded himself. After a few more drops slipped onto the cobbled walkway the wound sealed itself. Any remnants on the pavement vanished entirely. Undeterred, Ares conjured his sword—a broad, iridescent red blade—intent on carving the human into pieces.

Apollo's strong grip kept Ares restrained, preventing him approaching Zion again. Seething, Ares erupted into an inferno, scorching the nearby structures and vegetation. With a weary sigh and a casual wave, Hera quelled the flames.

"We must return to Olympus. Lingering here risks the very fabric of the universe. The convergence of his and our powers could unravel barriers that confine beings we are not prepared to face." Hera advised, her gaze lingering on Zion before she vanished, returning to Olympus. Her heart ached with the weight of sorrow for both him and the husband she had lost.

Apollo's turned his attention to Hades, who still lingered in the shadows. " Uncle, it appears something troubles you deeply." Disregarding his question, Hades stared coldly at Zion. A soft, seductive voice whispered in his ear, urging him to seize the opportunity.

"All that power could be yours. You should have been the ruler of the Olympians. Claim what is rightfully yours, Hades. Seize it. End him," the voice tempted Hades.

Enthralled by the seductive voice, Hades felt his hand rising slowly. Delving into the deepest recesses of his powers, Hades uttered the incantation in the ancient language of the gods.

"Natus tenebris aeternis, ego Hades dominus mortuorum. Te remitto in aeternam noctem et tuam potentiam sicut meam sumo,"— *Born of darkness eternal I Hades lord of the dead. Send you back into the eternal night and take your power as my own."* he spoke with a resonance that echoed through the divine realm.

The words, born of darkness eternal, were a proclamation of his sovereignty as the lord of the dead. Just as Hades was on the precipice of unleashing the magic, a delicate hand, small yet commanding, encircled his wrist. Snapping him out of the trance. A voice, stern and familiar, cut through the mystical haze.

"Hades, what were you thinking? We do not invoke such powers for selfish reasons," admonished Nike, the goddess of victory. Hades allowed his hand to be lowered. His chest heaved as he struggled to comprehend what had just transpired. Her gaze unwavering as she observed Hades grappling to regain control. She threw a vicious glare over her shoulder at Apollo.

"Get him out of here now!"

Swiftly, he placed a reassuring hand on Hades' shoulder before teleporting them both to Olympus. Nike stood unmoving, ensuring their presence had vanished before she could finally draw a breath. Falling to her knees, her entire being shook. She had narrowly averted catastrophe. Fury surged within her. What was Hera thinking bringing Ares and Hades. She had nearly cost Zion his life. Looking down she smiled at how handsome he was. All the anger drained right out of her. His smooth almond skin stretched tightly over lean muscle. His curly black bangs pooled over his eyes. He kept it trimmed closely on the sides. She ran her hands through his curls, enjoying the soft texture.

" Zion, I know you're tired of fighting for people who didn't fight for you. But I need you to be strong just a little longer. Don't give up just yet." she whispered to his unconscious body.

Scooping him up into her arms. As if she carried a small child she soared above the clouds. Cold air whipped around her face. She clutched Zion to her tightly to her chest. Her heart pounded fiercely against her rib cage. The feel of him in her arms sent jolts of electricity through her body. Angling towards the south of the city. She headed to the one place she knew he hated. Soaring through the open window leading to his room. She gently laid him down, and she used her powers to pull the blankets over him.

She knew she should leave immediately, but warring with herself. His lips, full and partially parted while he slept, seemed soft and inviting. Part of her wondered how they would feel pressed to hers. Biting her lower lip, she closed the few steps separating them. Her heart pounding loudly in her ears the closer her lips were to his. Hands shaking ever so slightly with trepidation. She brushed her hands against his cheek. His warm breath blew softly across her face. The enticing faint smell of peppermint reached her nose.

She placed the tiniest kiss on his lips so as not to wake him. Savoring the sweet velvety texture and taste of his lips Nike took a deep, unsteady breath. Before reluctantly pulling away from his lips. She watched as he rolled over, whispering her name.

"Nike."

Nike watched him as he continued to sleep as if he hadn't just absorbed the power of Zeus. The longer she stared at Zion the desire to be close to him grew stronger. She folded her wings and laid gently next to him resting her head on his chest. The powerful beats of his heart helped her drift off to sleep.

"I don't believe in destiny; I just do what's best for me." Zion's alarm echoed around the room.

As he rolled over to reach his phone his arm bumped into a soft figure. Sleeping next to him, the first word that came to mind was an angel, but an angel wasn't strong enough. No, she was a goddess. The armor she wore adorned her delicate form gleamed with a brilliance that rivaled the stars above, each metal plate shimmering in the radiant beams of the celestial moon. The moon's tender caress traced intricate patterns upon the polished surface, weaving a tapestry of tales that spoke of courage and triumph in the face of insurmountable odds. As she slept, an ethereal glow suffused her form.

Her presence was mesmerizing. In the few breaths that he stared at her he saw not only the goddess past the warrior, to the woman underneath it all. She small and fragile and in her slumber, power radiated from her that scared him. Moving slowly, he tried to extract himself from her toned body woven so intimately around his own. He was almost free when her eyes flew open. Moving faster than humanly possible she flipped him over pinning him down with one hand.

Wild glowing white eyes stared at him lost in a daze. Slowly she seemed to gather herself and relax. But her hand stayed pressed tightly against his throat. Feebly he tried to pry her hand away, but he would have better luck lifting a house than moving her hand. At least with the house Zion could use a wrecking ball. Doubtful even that would get her to budge. Waving his hand frantically reminding her that she was still choking him. Tears filled his eyes as he desperately gulped air into his starving lungs.

"Do you always try to kill people for trying to get away from you? Or is it just the ones whose house broke into?"

"No, sometimes I torture them before I strangle them." Nike laughed at the horrified expression on his face. Zion scooted away from her just in case she wasn't joking. Amusement danced in Nike's silver swirling eyes. She was tempted to yell boo to see how far he would jump.

"I'm not going to hurt you, Zion. I'm here to help you."

END

ARES BLOOD AND CHAOS

Arion stood once more in the forest that had woven itself into the fabrics of all his dreams. His heartbeat wildly as he searched for the figure that appeared every night. He scanned the base of each tall tree until he saw her. A glimmer glowing harlequin- green hair trailing behind her. As she moved gracefully from tree to tree. A fleeting vision of olive skin and a white gown spun and vanished only to reappear a few paces ahead. He tore after her pumping his legs reverently. He had to catch her this time. Whenever he had tried to get close before she vanished into the shadowy depths of the forest. Blending in with the thick foliage. Tonight, there was an electric charge to the forest. It thrummed and pulsed as if it was a slumbering beast. Luring its prey into well-laid trap.

Arion continued to chase after her, but she continued to stay just out of his reach. She seemed to glide across the earth each blade of grass propelling her forward. Ahead of him she stopped suddenly. Chest heaving Arion stopped as well trying to catch his breath. He watched as she lifted her hands in slow wide arc above her head. Readying herself for the beginning of what seemed a complex dance. Throwing her head back she laughed before launching into a series of movements. Twisting her limbs in a way that Arion didn't think was humanly possible. The trees around them swayed following her movements. Above them the skye grew dark as the moon made its way to across the sun. Bringing with it a crisp chilling air. Arion shivered as his body adjusted to the drop in temperature.

An ear-piercing screech echoed through the trees. A golden eagle soared over head challenging the other flying creatures for the title of Lord of the skye. His eyes focused back on Gaea. She was lost to a melody only she could hear. Her body as fluid and free as the wind flowing through the branches. It all reminded Arion of flower petals dancing in the wind. The rhythmic sway of her hips caused sparks of red and gold to explode around her. The light wound itself into a sphere of swirling colors. Images of boy no older than eight came into sharpened as her body moved faster. He emerged out of pyre of fire. His eyes matching the dancing flames. Shifting from red to yellow before settling on a mix of the two colors. His blonde hair hung loosely down his back. He looked oddly familiar. Arion couldn't quite place where he had seen him. It was an annoying itch he couldn't scratch. The boy's eyes held a strange hunger and desire that called out to Arion. Gingerly he took a step forward. But the image changed.

A small fissure formed in the middle of a volcano. Lava sprayed out in different directions. Burning away any traces of all it touched. A large brown hand shot out of the lava pulling away large chunks of charred earth. Arion watched in awe. Unlike the boy's birth this man's wasn't easy. He continued to claw until he made a hole large enough to pull himself through. His broad shoulders rolled and flexed as he stood to full height. He was a mountain of a man. Small patches of his thick black beard caught fire. Unfazed he raised one massive hand to pat the flames out. His eyes were unnerving, the left a bright orange glowed like the dying embers of a fire. Tiny speckle of brown floated around the iris. The right was the inverse of his left eye. A deep rich russet-brown with orange flecks of color. He raised a hand towards Gaea and Arion. Trying to reach through the roving sphere of colors. Only to pull back at the last second.

Gaea twirled her hands summoning a second identical sphere. Side by side the images of the two beings floated. The edges of the two spheres brushed against each other. Sending a wave of shearing heat powerful enough. Arion felt it even though he was still several feet away. Cosmic energy arched and surged around Gaea, Taking a life of its own. It reached out where the two spheres connected. Twisting violently through the air. Arion shielded his eyes as he was temporarily blinded. Dark spots danced across his vision as the light folded in on itself. In place of the brilliant light stood a woman, a soft pink glow emanating from her. Beneath her feet remnants of scorched earth. A perfect blend of the two warring elements. Petite and frail like a dainty new flower, volcanic energy simmered beneath the surface. Obsidian, springy curls framed her slender shoulders, an orange streak fell down the left side of her face. Deep electrifying fuchsia stared directly at him. Studying Arion, the same way he studied her. Full round lips parted in the cutest frown.

Gaea turned to face him. "Look Arion, look at our family." she beamed. "It's small for now, but the others will come." He glanced back at the figures behind her pausing on *fire-boy*. He stared pointedly at Arion waiting for him to finally understand. He cocked his head to the side in a manner so familiar. Arion finally realized who he was staring at. His younger self smiled wool-fully at him. The details of his birth came rushing back to him. How had he forgotten? Behind him branches snapped as something large barreled towards them. A herd of frightened deer erupted into the clearing. Their eyes wild with panic. Eager to get away from whatever had them spooked. The antlers of a large male deer caught him in the stomach. Doubling over he clutched his stomach. More of the scared animals smacked into him.

Lost in a thunder of hooves and fur. Arion jolted out of the bed. Trying to avoid the hooves he imagined were still coming towards him. Breathing hard he stared wide eyed searching. At the edges of his vision miniature flames wove themselves into his blanket. Feeding on the thick wool. The acrid smell of burning *felt* clogged and filled his senses. Moving quickly, he fetched the bucket of water at the foot of his bed. He kept it full most nights just in case. *Great! Normal teenagers worried about wetting themselves in their sleep. He had to worry about setting the house on fire.* Tossing the water onto the small fires, Arion wondered if he would ever learn to control his power.

Ares blinked away the memories that clouded his vision. His human life had been centuries ago. He needed to focus on the battle unfolding before him. He stood on a high rise overlooking the men running back and forth. Had they looked up they might have caught a glimpse of him clad in his red and gold armor. But humans seldom thought outside of themselves. Over three hundred Spartan men readied themselves for battle. Each praying to him to save them. Except one, Leonidas the King of Sparta.

"Lord Ares, be with me in this battle. Sharpen my blade so that it may cut down my enemies. Accept the blood of my enemies as tribute for the victory to come. Let all of Olympus witness this gloriousness of this battle." He finished. Ares studied the man with an air of amusement. He would wait to see if the human was worthy of his help. The Persians advanced their numbers seemed endless compared to the tiny number of Spartans that remained. The clash of bronze, the screams of the dying, the earth drinking deep of mortal blood – it was a symphony to his ears. Surrounded, outnumbered, the Spartans fought with a savagery that was impressive. Their spears broke, so they fought with swords. When their swords shattered, they fought with their bare hands and teeth. Reveling in the mounting death toll, Ares watched on with interest. Leonidas laughing as he claimed the life of yet another Persian soldier. Withdrawing from the battle Ares felt the summoning from another mortal not among the men fighting for their lives. Curious he spread his consciousness to the woman beseeching him so fervently. "Lord Ares come to me. Hear my plea. Lord Ares. Lord Ares." Her voice echoed in his mind repeatedly. She was pretty enough for a mortal woman. Her brown curls tumbled around shoulders hiding her face from his view. Appearing in front of the altar which she prayed. Ares passed a less than amused expression over her.

"Why have you summoned me?"

The woman backed away at his sudden appearance. Her voice seeming to fail her for several seconds. "Speak human what did you summon me for?" Ares spat at her.

"My... My husband," she stammered. Quickly losing patience with the woman Ares stalked towards her with deadly strides. She backed away from him uncertain of his intentions. She barely made a few steps when her limbs locked in place. Her jerked up as Ares forced her to stare into his eyes. In an instant he knew her every thought. Releasing his hold on her Ares looked at Queen Gorgo. A spark of respect for the Spartan Queen. Her devotion to her husband had been visible in her mind. The amount of love she held for Leonidas forced his mind to recall another moment when he had been human.

Heartbroken and consumed by grief, he had beseeched Gaea, the mother of all, to restore his beloved. Once more he stood in the forest where the trees blotted out the sun. A place so familiar to him he could walk with his eyes closed and never trip. Gaea, her eyes filled with compassion, regarded him solemnly.

"I will grant your request, my son. But know this, the price to bring her back will be high."

Arion's heart clenched with anguish, but he nodded, his resolve unwavering.

"I'll do anything. Just bring her back," he begged falling to his knees.

He watched as Gaea began to move and sing in a language that was familiar yet foreign to him. Slowly out of the clay in front of them a figure started to form. The clay morphed and twisted to the melody of Gaea's voice. Iridescent, magenta curls cascaded around her slender shoulders, a fiery mixture of volcanic-watermelon and smoldering peach hues that radiated with the intensity of a sunset. Deep electrifying fuchsia stared directly at him. In the same manner they had stared so many years ago. Expect there was no fire in them this time. She regarded him with a detached cold expression. Excited he embraced her placing a chaste kiss on her scarlet lips. But her lips stayed frozen against his.

"My love," he whispered, his voice thick with emotion. "Do you remember me?"

"Thalassa it's me Arion," he pleaded desperately.

"Thalassa? I am Aphrodite." Her voice gentle and sweet cut through Arion's heart like tempered knife. Arion saw red as he spun to confront Gaea.

"What have you done?" She doesn't even know who I am or who she is." He spat.

"I did as you asked, I restored her, but remember I said there was price to pay." Gaea said. Her movements slow and graceful she stepped into his arms. Placing a delicate olive hand on his chest. Arion felt a slight tug in chest before pain ricocheted through his body. Clutching his still beating heart Gaea approached Aphrodite.

"With this she will be fully reborn. Filled with the fire of the one she loved." Aphrodite gasped as if she had been struck by lightning. Her body glowed with energy.

Arion's vision darkened. He felt as if he had been torn into thousand pieces. Inside him the fire raged and burned. No longer leashed and controlled it at him. But despite the pain he felt. Power pulsed through him flooding his body with rage and shaping him into something new.

Arion rose, his form wreathed in flames, his eyes burning with an unquenchable fury. His hair turned from blonde to crimson red a testament to the enduring power of love and the devastating cost of his loss. From that day forth, he became the embodiment of war, Ares the god of war. His every step marked by the thunderous clash of armies and the cries of the fallen.

Ares pulled his mind away from the past focusing on Queen Gorgo. His features now sober he put more distance between himself and the Queen of Sparta. He had not thought about Thalassa for centuries. Part of him hated the Queen for making him relive those memories. Without a word to her he returned to the battle just as thousands of arrows pierced Leonidas. He fell back amongst his men a smile on his lips, sword still in hand. Ares angry roar filled the valley. Raising his hand, he intended to splinter the Persians. But he knew the rules that governed them. He must not intervene with the mortals. So, he lowered his hand and watched the people he favored were slaughtered below him. Once again faced with the pain of being powerless.

END

ETERNAL SHADOWS

Athena stood on the summit of Olympus, her gaze sweeping across the majestic hills and ethereal beauty that defined the realm of the gods. The air shimmered with divine energy, and the golden glow of Olympus bathed her in its warm embrace. Yet, for Athena, the radiant splendor held a bittersweet taste. Rolling hills, adorned with celestial flora, seemed to etch itself into her memory. Athena's thoughts were a tempest of conflicting emotions as she contemplated the gravity of her impending journey into the heart of Tartarus. The beauty of Olympus, once a source of solace, now felt like a fleeting moment in the face of the impending darkness.

In the quiet stillness of the divine haven, Athena took a moment to center herself. The winds whispered secrets, and the distant echoes of immortal laughter filled the air. It was a tranquil scene, a deceptive calm before the storm. With a determined resolve, Athena descended from the heights of Olympus, her footsteps echoing through the marble halls. As she moved towards the edge of the divine realm, she cast one last longing glance at the hills, where the beauty of the gods' abode unfolded in all its grandeur.

The transition from the celestial splendor to the shadowy precipice was abrupt. The vibrant colors of Olympus faded into an abyss of eternal night. A sense of foreboding enveloped Athena as she ventured deeper into the realm where Nyx, the goddess of night, held sway. The path she treaded was not illuminated by divine radiance. Instead, she followed the subtle glow of her own wisdom. Along the way, she encountered ethereal barriers and spectral guardians, each challenging her resolve. Athena, relying on her strategic prowess, navigated the obstacles with a grace that mirrored the dance of constellations in the night sky.

Athena approached the Doors of Night, standing imposingly at the boundary between the mortal realm and the eternal shadows. She could feel Nyx's power pressing down on her. An aura of otherworldly staggering evil. Crafted from the obsidian essence of the cosmos. The Doors of Night colossal gates possessed an inherent darkness that seemed to absorb every trace of light. Intricate patterns, like that of constellations, etched into the surface. The tiny stars flared slightly before darkening.

The surface of the doors felt cool under pale hands. She shivered slightly the realm itself throbbed with icy energy. A soft, haunting hum filled the air, a harmonious resonance from the souls of the damned. Pulling the doors open Athena stepped into Nyx's throne room. Nyx. The goddess of night, draped in an ethereal sheer gown sat on her ebony throne. She regarded Athena her gaze neutral. The clash of their powers seared the air in front of them. Causing it snap and crackle.

"I've come for Aphrodite," Athena demanded.

Nyx raised an eyebrow, betraying neither surprise nor concern. Her eyes infinite pools of ebony -black holes swam with amusement.

"Have you now?" She laughed.

With a wave of her hand Aphrodite appeared before them kneeling in chains. Golden blood dripped from several wounds on her body. Nyx yanked the chain holding her, forcing a muffled cry of pain from her. Tears welled in her eyes as she tried to silently plea for her freedom. Athena, undeterred, stepped forward, the echo of her footsteps reverberating through the celestial chamber. Her armor gleaming with the brilliance of starlight appeared covering her body. She unsheathed her bronze celestial sword. Light rippled down the spine of the blade.

"The balance has been disrupted long enough Nyx. Release her."

Shadows swirled around Nyx like a tempest. From the darkness emerged twin obsidian daggers, their edges whispered of never-ending night. Nyx's eyes glowed, and the very essence of shadows danced covering her. She swirled vanishing before Athena's eyes. Concealed by the shadows she struck out aiming for Athena's throat. Athena parried the dagger and kicked her back. Their blades met and clashed as Athena strategically countered Nyx's every move.

For the briefest, moment they were evenly matched. Each swing of Athena's sword and twist of Nyx's daggers left an imprint on the very essence of the divine realm. The clash of their powers painted the air with vibrant hues. The scent of ionized energy filled the room. A heady mix of cosmic radiance and the faintest trace of the shadows that Nyx commanded. A symphony of crackling celestial energy, akin to the rustling of millions chattering birds echoed around them.

Athena's mercury eyes flicked towards Aphrodite. The glance cost her as Nyx sliced open her arm. Sticky warm golden blood trailed down her arm. The wound festered and turned black. Switching hands Athena drove Nyx back. Her blade flashing in a dangerous combination nearly beheading Nyx. While she battled her mind calculated a strategy.

"Come now Athena. Where was that bravado you showed gone?" Nyx taunted. Athena ignored her knowing that the slightest distraction could mean her life. Spinning with an unparalleled grace, Athena directed a surge of energy toward the shackles ensnaring Aphrodite. The shadows that bound her sister crumbled away, dissolving into nothingness. As Aphrodite stepped free, Athena swayed, her once luminous form flickered like a waning star. Nyx's obsidian dagger protruding through her chest plate.

Rushing forward Aphrodite caught Athena before her body could hit the ground. Athena's breaths came in labored gasps. Despite her weakened state, her eyes held a glint of unwavering resolve. "Aphrodite, go," she whispered, her voice a mere echo of its former strength.

Aphrodite, tears glistening in her eyes, hesitated. "I won't leave you, Athena. We can find a way—"

No," Athena interrupted, placing a gentle hand on Aphrodite's cheek. "The balance demands this. I've given you a chance us all a chance." With her last breath, Athena turned her gaze to Nyx. "You will fail, Zion is stronger than you think he is. The threads of fate cannot be manipulated as easily."

With a final, weary smile, Athena's luminosity faded. The energy that once pulsed through her dissipated into the cosmic winds. Her body turning to vapor. The essence of wisdom, released, returned to the fabric of the universe.

END

ABOUT THE AUTHOR

W.E. Hampton, an up-and-coming novelist, captivates audiences with his creative works in various genres that span across fiction, fantasy, adventure, and new age literature. Currently pursuing a Bachelor Degree of Fine Arts in Creative Writing at Full Sail University, Hampton is dedicated to improving his storytelling abilities and broadening his literary repertoire. Hampton's literary pursuits extend beyond academics. His poetic skills are showcased in his published work, "Casual Meeting," which was released through Silent Spark Press. An active participant in the literary community, Hampton remains engaged and informed through memberships with Silent Spark Press and Query Tracker. Aside from his writing Hampton draws inspiration form the fantastical worlds found in books, filled with superheroes, gods, dragons, and wizards. Whether dreaming of attending Hogwarts, soaring through the skies, or embarking on a quest, Hampton's passion for fantastical storytelling ignites his creative imagination.

Linked In: https://www.linkedin.com/in/will-hampton-35456b303/

Facebook:https://www.facebook.com/willhampton21?mibextid=LQQJ4d&rdid=UwU993kGROAcvAgF